GLADIATOR BOY

BOY

vs

THE INSANE FURY

Win an exclusive
Gladiator Boy T-shirt and goody bag!

Use the special code below to decode the sentence, then send it in to us.
Each month we will draw one winner to receive a Gladiator Boy T-shirt
and goody bag.

THE INSANE FURY

DAVID GRIMSTONE

*Hodder
Children's
Books*

A division of Hachette Children's Books

Typeset by Tony Fleetwood

Printed and bound in the UK by CPI Bookmarque, Croydon, CR0 4TD

The paper and board used in this paperback by Hodder Children's Books are
natural recyclable products made from wood grown in
sustainable forests. The manufacturing processes conform to the
environmental regulations of the country of origin.

Hodder Children's Books
a division of Hachette Children's Books
338 Euston Road, London NW1 3BH
An Hachette UK company

www.hachette.co.uk

*For James 'Jay' Bugden, for bringing
the awesome Karkin Vetch to life.*

*This new series is dedicated to Leilani Sparrow,
who has worked tirelessly with Gladiator Boy
since his arrival. Thanks also to Anne McNeil,
who has stood in my corner since day one.*

HOW MANY OF

GLADIATOR BOY

SERIES ONE HAVE YOU COLLECTED?

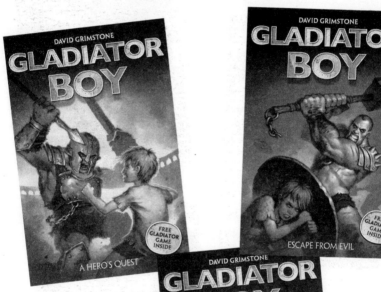

DAVID GRIMSTONE

GLADIATOR BOY

THE REBELS' ASSAULT

FREE GLADIATOR GAME INSIDE

DAVID GRIMSTONE

GLADIATOR BOY

THE BLADE OF FIRE

FREE GLADIATOR GAME INSIDE

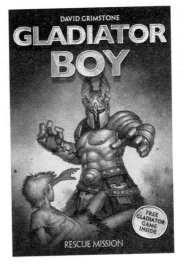

DAVID GRIMSTONE

GLADIATOR BOY

RESCUE MISSION

FREE GLADIATOR GAME INSIDE

CHINA

PREVIOUSLY IN GLADIATOR BOY

Badly injured during a battle with the deadly Aritezu, Decimus Rex lies dying on the hills of Yelang. Meanwhile, the other slaves manage to defeat the two remaining ninjas and force them into submission. Unfortunately, Ruma is infected by a red powder blown into his face during the combat . . .

CHAPTER
I

CAPTURED

Decimus Rex was wounded. He couldn't tell how bad the wounds were or how deeply the ninja's discs had plunged into his flesh . . . but he knew he was bleeding, and he could feel the cold creeping over him as he drifted in and out of consciousness.

The last few years of his life flashed before his eyes in graphic detail; images of fighting in the arena, leaping platforms and running over coals, the sea voyage with Olu, the battle at Suvius Tower. Even the adventure beneath Arena Primus with the monster known as the Maw now seemed so hard to believe in the plain light of day . . . then a voice punctuated the dreams. At first, he thought it might be the voice of the gods, or even his own thoughts, but then he recognized the familiar tone.

'Decimus! Oh no; Decimus, you can't
be dead!'

His vision swam as he slowly blinked in the
bright light of the sun; Gladius was kneeling
beside him, his hands supporting the base of his
neck.

'That's it! Open your eyes! Can you hear me?'

Decimus tried to speak, but all that would emerge from his throat was a weak croak. He summoned all his energy and tried again.

'Ninja,' he managed. 'Dead. He . . . got me . . . with—'

'You're still bleeding badly, Decimus. I've ripped up some of my tunic to stem the flow, but I'm going to need the others to help me . . . I can't drag you along in this state – you need lifting completely. We have to get you back to Tonino's boat – he might know what to do. Hold on, Decimus! Please hold on!'

The voice faded, and Gladius's friendly face swam away as if it had never existed. Once again Decimus was plunged into a dream-world that seemed to consist entirely of his own memories.

This time, the pictures moved more slowly . . .
and he found himself hovering above them,
watching like a spectator as he arrived at the
Winter Palace, struggled through the water
maze and fought Tekaro in the dark.

So many amazing things had happened to him
. . . could this really be the end of his journey?

Slavious Doom rested on the balcony of the
Winter Palace and looked out over the
surrounding landscape. His face was troubled,
and dark shadows encircled his eyes.

Behind him, King D'Tong emerged from
the throne room and shuffled out to meet
his co-conspirator.

'Not worry, Doom Lord,' said the old man. 'My ninjas highly trained; will kill them all.'

Slavious removed his great demon helmet, and slowly shook his head.

'No,' he said. 'I have changed my mind. Decimus Rex has humiliated me – both at home, and here. He must die in my own country, not here, thousands of miles away where only a handful of my servants will know. I want my people to see him suffer.'

A look of panic suddenly gripped the face of the king.

'But my ninjas . . . they—'

'Send more guards,' Doom snapped. 'Have them called back – I don't care what happens to the other slaves; just make sure Decimus is brought to me alive . . . and in good condition. I

will return to Rome with that wretch in chains . . .
my revenge will be taken in the public forum.'

D'Tong held up a hand. 'Doom Lord; you must—'

'I must nothing!' screamed the overlord,
turning on the king with blazing eyes full of
malice. 'I might remind you that you only have
your royal prisoner because of my assistance.
Soon, I must return to my own land . . . and our
alliance will only end peacefully if we both have
what we want. I hope you understand me . . .'

'But other boy—'

'The other boy was my prisoner anyway – you
were only holding him here for me. You surely
can't expect any reward for that?'

King D'Tong muttered under his breath, but
couldn't summon the courage to argue aloud.
Instead, he bowed his head and summoned a

team of his most agile guards to go out in pursuit
of the ninjas.

More images sailed through the mind of
Decimus Rex, this time of guards wearing
unfamiliar armour, lifting him from the ground
and carrying him off toward the mountains.

Decimus couldn't tell whether this was
actually happening to him or if it was merely
another part of his ongoing dreams, but he was
too weak to struggle either way. The sky flashed
past above him, appearing as a brief glimpse of
blue every time his eyes flicked open.

The air whistled in his ears, and he heard
distant voices in a language he recognized but

didn't fully understand.

Time passed . . . very quickly.

Gladius reached the brow of the hill and
stopped dead.

'He's gone! Decimus? Decimus!'

Without another word to
his companions, Gladius hurtled
down the hillside, losing his
footing at one point and
sliding for several feet
on his back through
the dirt.

Olu and Argon hurried after him; only Ruma followed at an unconcerned pace.

'Maybe he got up and walked away?' said the scrawny Etrurian, glancing around at the hills.

'Impossible!' Gladius yelled back, coming to a halt at the base of the hill and indicating patches of ground where the blood had soaked through. 'He wasn't in any state to walk anywhere! They've taken him! They must have taken him!'

Ruma continued to stare down at the ground.

'Who exactly?' he asked. 'We tied up two of the ninjas and you said Decimus killed the other one. Who else is there?'

'D'Tong's guards, of course! He sent the ninjas after us on Doom's orders; maybe he second guessed himself and dispatched a group of soldiers as back-up.'

Ruma shrugged, and started down the ridge towards them.

'Why didn't they just finish Decimus off if he was dying, anyway?'

Gladius darted an angry glance at the Etrurian.

'What's wrong with you, Ruma?'

'No, he's right,' said Olu, carefully. 'From what Ruma told us, it doesn't make any sense for them to take him anywhere. Doom and D'Tong tried to kill you in the water maze, then sent those ninjas to finish the job when you escaped.'

Gladius stood up and straightened his jaw, defiantly.

'Maybe Doom wanted to see him die? You

remember what an evil, twisted ogre he is?'

'So where do you think they've taken Decimus?' Argon wondered.

Gladius looked back toward the forest, his lips trembling with sudden anger.

'The Winter Palace,' he muttered. 'That's where Doom has set up his base.'

'Then that's where we're going,' said Olu, clapping one hand on Gladius's shoulder and giving his friend a supportive squeeze. 'We will find him.'

'Yes,' Argon agreed, throwing an arm around him too. 'If Decimus is still alive, we will save him . . . as he would have done for us. If he's not, well, we'll rescue him and bring him home.'

'What's the use of rescuing a corpse?' put in Ruma. 'We'll all end up captured. We should think of ourselves and go home while we can. We could kill those ninjas we captured on the way back.'

A grim silence settled on the group as all eyes turned to look at the Etrurian. He was standing on the dusty ground with arms folded and a nonplussed expression on his face.

Gladius and Olu both wanted to shout an answer to the question, but it was Argon who spoke first . . . in a heavy, rather pained voice.

'What was in that red dust, I wonder?' he said, moving over to Ruma and looking his friend directly in the eye. 'You haven't been yourself since you got hit with it.'

Ruma twitched slightly in the heat of the Gaul's glare, but smiled back nevertheless.

'I'm fine,' he growled back. 'I just think it's

dangerous to forget about those two surviving ninjas, that's all – they won't stay tied up for long.'

'We go after Decimus,' said Olu, with equal fervour. 'And that's all there is to it.'

Gladius and Argon both nodded in agreement, but Ruma merely shrugged and followed them sulkily as they made their way back to the forest path.

Decimus awoke, cold. He wasn't sure how long he'd been unconscious or how near he'd come to dying ... but he knew he felt better.

Raising his head slightly, he saw that his wounds were covered with clean white bandages and that his battered body had been washed and cleaned. His first thought was that Gladius had managed to rescue him. However, the sense of relief he felt quickly vanished when he realized he was chained to an icy slab of stone in what appeared to be a subterranean cell of some sort.

No, he soon realized that 'cell' was definitely the wrong word. This place was more like a vast underground dungeon. He knew instinctively that he was inside the Winter Palace.

Decimus turned his head slightly and tried to shift his body on the slab. He couldn't move very much, however, and the dungeon was poorly illuminated, with only a few flaming torches adorning the bare stone walls.

'Is . . . anyone there?' he called, angry at the fear and weakness in his voice.

There was movement in the far corner of the

dungeon, and Decimus felt suddenly stupid for making a noise: he was in no state to fight, and he seriously doubted the hall contained anything but armed guards.

The shadows in the room lengthened, and a figure half emerged from the darkness, its slow and cautious movement accompanied by the distinctive rattle of chains.

'Are you another prisoner?' he called, squinting into the darkness. 'Are you chained up like me? Gladius; is that you, old friend?'

Decimus knew the answer to his question immediately; the other prisoner definitely wasn't Gladius.

Standing in the pool of light cast by one of the flaming torches was the most beautiful girl Decimus had ever seen in his life. She was small

and slender with dark hair that was plastered to

her face with grime. It seemed to Decimus that

she must have been in the dungeon for a long

time: the rags that she wore were tattered and

29

faded, and the chain around her ankle did little to obscure several dark bruises earned in what must have been a desperate attempt to break free.

As she edged across the floor towards him, the chain became more and more taut. Eventually, it stopped her progress completely . . . several feet away from where he was lying.

Despite the fact that the girl was obviously a native of China, Decimus tried to communicate with her in the hope that she might understand some of his own language.

'What is your name?' he said, trying to study her expression. 'How long have you been here?'

The girl remained motionless, and she made no effort to reply.

'I am Decimus Rex,' he continued, feeling stupid. 'Decimus – my name.' He was racking his brains to remember his brief conversation with the old map-seller, but he couldn't recall a single word or phrase she'd said; too much had happened since.

'Did the king put you down here?' he went on. 'King D'Tong?'

Finally, a look of recognition appeared on the girl's porcelain face. She nodded, very slightly, and indicated the chains around her legs . . . but, still, she said nothing.

'My friends and I came here to rescue someone,' he said, almost feeling foolish for continuing to talk when he knew she couldn't understand him. 'But we got lured into a trap. Instead of finding Teo, we found Slavio—'

'Teo?'

The girl's voice rang out in the dungeon so

loudly that it actually caused Decimus to start.

'Teo?' he said again, hopefully.

The girl smiled and pointed past the slab on which Decimus was lying. It took every ounce of effort the young gladiator possessed in order for him to twist himself around and look behind him.

There, in a rusty iron cage suspended from a hook on the ceiling, was Teo.

Battered, bruised, weak and unconscious ... but very definitely alive.

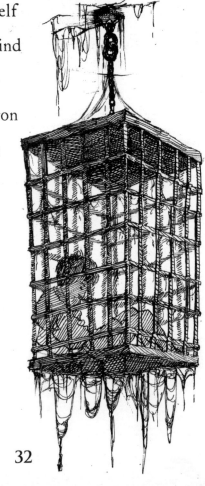

CHAPTER II

ASSAULT ON THE PALACE

Midnight arrived in Yelang, and a pale moon was visible in the sky. A series of paper lanterns lined the gardens of the Winter Palace, working together to throw up a gentle pool of light that bathed the base of the building and left the towering spires outlined against the dark sky.

On the edge of the palace gardens, Gladius poked his head out of a low hedge and surveyed the scene.

'Three guards,' he whispered. 'Two guarding the side entrance and one on patrol around the borders.'

Behind him, Argon and Olu nodded. Ruma muttered something under his breath.

'I say we split up,' Gladius continued. 'Argon, you can handle the one that's moving; the rest of us will take the two sentries. Agreed? Good. Let's go!'

The boys divided. Olu, Gladius and Ruma crept along behind the hedge while Argon simply stayed put: the guard on patrol was heading his way, a vacant expression on his face and a heavy-looking staff in his arms.

Argon counted under his breath. Three. Two. One. NOW.

He leapt from the side of the hedge and barrelled into the man, who was thankfully a good head shorter than him. They both rolled on to the ground, but Argon was on his feet first. Somersaulting over the body of the struggling guard, he ripped off the guard's helmet and delivered a powerful chop to the back of the man's neck.

The guard went face first into the dirt, but didn't lose consciousness. Scrambling madly to get back on to his feet, he seized the staff and tried to lift it from the ground. Argon quickly helped, bringing the staff up so it was right under the guard's chin. Then, dragging on it with all his might, Argon began to choke the little man into unconsciousness, careful to release the weapon the second he felt his enemy relax.

The guard sagged noticeably, and Argon hauled him into the bushes. It was only then that a startling idea occurred to him . . . and he quickly donned the man's uniform.

Gladius was about halfway to the side entrance of the Winter Palace before he realized that someone was missing.

'Where's Ruma?' he hissed at Olu, pausing before he reached the end of trees: another step and they would emerge into the pool of light thrown up by the lanterns.

Olu glanced around him.

'He was here five seconds ago,' he whispered. 'I just asked him to watch my back!'

Gladius peered along the route they had taken from the borders of the garden, but there was no sign of the scrawny Etrurian.

'I don't like this one bit,' Olu admitted. 'Something bad has happened to Ruma – I think that dust must have seriously affected his mind or something . . .'

Gladius sighed.

'We'll just have to deal with the sentries by ourselves,' he muttered. 'We can try to find Ruma when the coast is clear.'

Olu nodded, and the pair crept forward.

The sentries on duty were evidently not among King D'Tong's best men. One was asleep, standing up, while the other seemed completely fascinated by an insect that was crawling across the top of his staff.

Olu stunned Gladius with what he did next. Without another word to his companion, he simply strode out of the shadows and punched the distracted guard straight in the face. A look of shocked surprise quickly disappeared as the guard folded up and collapsed to the ground.

Taken aback, Gladius almost missed his opportunity for attack and would undoubtedly have suffered for it had his own opponent not been waking up from a very deep slumber. The clumsy, inept guard made a desperate lunge for his staff, but his vision was obviously still blurred as he missed the weapon entirely ... giving Gladius the chance to snatch the staff from him and drive the edge under his chin with considerable force.

It was only when the second guard had dropped that Gladius saw the approaching danger.

'Olu!' he cried. 'Look out! Behind you!'

The boy turned as quickly as he could, but wasn't in time to avoid a third guard, who had appeared from nowhere and leapt on to the steps

beside them. Instinctively, Olu brought up both
hands in order to protect himself, while Gladius
made a lunge for the new attacker . . . missing by
a mile.

The guard watched them both scramble
around on the floor before removing his helmet

and grinning at them.

'The disguise works, then,' he said. 'I thought it might. Where's Ruma?'

Gladius and Olu gawped at Argon, but neither could speak for a moment.

'You two should try to take their uniforms,' the Gaul continued, indicating the unconscious sentries. He glanced over at Gladius. 'Yours might be a squeeze, but it's still worth trying. If we enter the palace as guards, we're likely to be able to move around freely.'

He helped both boys to their feet.

'Where is Ruma, exactly?'

Olu shrugged, and stared out over the palace gardens. 'He went off somewhere.'

'Olu asked him to watch our backs,' Gladius added. 'I suppose he thought he could do that from a distance. To be honest, I can't tell what's going on in Ruma's head, at the moment. It's almost like he's gone completely mad.'

The two slaves quickly exchanged outfits with the prone guards, and Argon helped them to drag the men into the bushes at the base of the steps.

'Shouldn't one of us go and look for Ruma?' Olu hazarded, as they prepared to enter the palace.

Gladius shook his head. 'Decimus may be dead, or dying. At least we know Ruma is OK – we won't leave the palace without him, but I don't think he should be our first priority. Do you?'

Argon nodded in agreement, and the three friends quickly entered the Winter Palace.

'Teo,' said Decimus loudly, trying to keep the disbelief from his voice and fighting against his chains in order to point at the sleeping prisoner. 'He is Teo.' Then he moved his hand back to his own chest and tapped it, twice. 'Decimus,' he said slowly, watching the girl for any hint of recognition. 'Decimus. Who are you?'

This time, he got a nod in reply.

'Akina,' said the girl, in a voice that sounded like it hadn't been used for many days. She looked down at her chains with a mixture of sorrow and anger. 'Akina.'

'She . . . princess.'

Decimus started in shock, and craned his neck around once again.

Teo was awake, and smiling weakly.

'Dessmus,' he said, shifting slightly in the swinging cage. 'Hello ... Dessmus.'

A million thoughts rushed through the young gladiator's mind as he struggled to find the right words: he still couldn't believe Teo was alive ... after all this time.

'What you do here?' Teo asked, raising one bloodied eyebrow. 'Much danger ... Doom.'

'I know!' Decimus cried, trying and failing to stop himself from blurting out everything that was on his mind. 'We've seen the evil maggot! How come you're talking all of a sudden? You never used to say anything! We came out here to rescue you, Teo! I thought it was all a trap, but we couldn't risk the possibility that you might be ... argghgh ... how did you survive the noose? I saw you die, Teo: I saw you dead. We all did! I can't believe it was you who sent that message . . .'

Teo shook his head.

'No send message,' he said, darkly. 'Doom. Trap. Use me . . . get you.'

Decimus nodded, but he couldn't share the prisoner's mood: he was so glad to see that Teo was alive and, if not well, then at least capable of speaking. It was a miracle!

'Did you say she was a princess?' Decimus said, suddenly remembering the first words Teo had spoken when he awoke.

Teo did not reply immediately, but spoke to the girl in his own language first. The two exchanged some sort of careful conversation before any reply was ventured.

'She . . . Princess Akina . . . daughter . . . Grand

King . . . Emperor.'

Decimus tried to sit up on the slab, but managed just a few precious inches of movement.

'Why does King D'Tong have the Emperor's daughter chained up inside his palace?' he said, his face creased in puzzlement.

Another exchange took place between Akina and Teo. Then the boy spoke once more.

'He use her . . . get throne.'

A knowing look flashed in the young gladiator's eyes. 'So he's trying to overthrow the Emperor here – the same thing Doom is attempting to do back home. Well, we will have to stop them both, won't we?'

With a roar of furious anger, Decimus heaved against his chains, spending every last ounce of strength in an effort to get them to shift, even slightly.

'It no use,' said Teo, sadly. 'Chains here strong. We stay long time.'

'Never,' Decimus growled, his eyes flashing with a new fire. 'Never.'

Argon marched boldly past three armed guards and headed off along a plush new corridor. Behind him, Gladius and Olu tried to keep time by marching in step with the Gaul.

'When it comes to disguises,' said Argon, when it turned out that the new passage was deserted, 'there are two important things to remember. The first is to always look confident and the second is never to look like you don't know where you're going. Now – THIS WAY.'

The trio marched on, rounding two new bends in the corridor before striding determinedly towards the end of a third – even more luxurious-looking – passage.

'One thing, Argon,' Olu whispered, as Gladius fiddled with his uncomfortable uniform for the hundredth time. 'It goes without saying that if Decimus is alive, he's in the dungeons – right?'

The Gaul nodded.

'Right . . . so, if we're searching for the dungeons, shouldn't we be heading away from the decorative part of the palace?'

'Of course we should,' Gladius snapped, as the clasp on his helmet snapped open. 'What we're looking for is bare stone walls and flaming torches . . . not purple drapes and

brightly coloured paintings!'

Argon was about to agree when a loud voice rang out from the far end of the corridor.

'Dûng yí xià!'

A guard had emerged from a side-room and was hurrying towards them. Admittedly, he looked more like a man furious with his servants than one who had discovered intruders, but Argon wasn't keen to take any chances. The Gaul simply stood his ground, and motioned for the others to do the same.

'Dûng yí xià!' came the voice again, as the guard drew closer. 'N? jiào shénme?'

Argon nodded obediently, picked up his staff and marched towards the man in a smart, orderly fashion. Gladius and Olu both hung back, waiting to see what their inspired friend would do when addressed in a language none of them understood.

'N? jiào shénme?' the guard repeated, but he didn't get to utter the question a third time.

Argon snapped to attention in front of him, eyes staring directly ahead. However, instead of facing whatever punishment the man had in mind, he suddenly darted forward and drove his head directly into the guard's chin, dropping him like a sack of potatoes and catching him bodily before he hit the ground.

Gladius and Olu quickly returned to the junction to check for any further attention as Argon carried the senior guard into the room from which he had originally emerged.

When he returned to the group, the three of them headed off along a new corridor.

'That was amazing,' Gladius admitted. 'Even I thought you were going to try to bluff your way past him.'

Argon smiled, and shrugged.

'This way looks more promising,' Olu whispered, pointing along a new corridor. 'No floor coverings, and the walls are damp.'

They moved off into the depths of the palace.

CHAPTER III

PRISONERS

There was a problem . . . a very, very big problem.

Having searched the Winter Palace for several hours, it appeared that the only way to get to the dungeon was through the palace kitchen, and in the kitchen . . . was a cook.

Argon just stopped where he was standing, his jaw slack and his eyes bulging in their sockets. Olu and Gladius had to drag him back around the corner before he gave them away.

'What is it?' asked Olu. 'What's wrong?'

Gladius didn't wait for the Gaul to answer. Instead, he forced his way to the edge of the wall and peered around the corner himself.

'Oh my gods,' he said, his face sagging with disbelief, 'that is the biggest man I have ever seen in my life. How in the name of mercy are we supposed to get past him?'

Olu swapped places with his friend, and took a look himself.

The man was wearing an apron, and very little else. It was difficult to tell if this was because it was so stiflingly hot in the kitchen, or if he had simply burst every last stitch of

clothing he'd ever worn. He sat at a table dishing out small bowls of meat from a large, cauldron-shaped pot that stood on the floor beside him. Olu noticed with increasing dismay that he didn't simply take up several spaces at the table; he took up one complete side of the table. If anything was certain, it was that all three of them together wouldn't stand a chance against this mountain of flesh. 'Can't we just act confident if he stops us?' Gladius whispered. 'That's what Argon did with the guard upstairs . . . well, at first. We're in uniform, remember?'

'Yeah,' said Olu. 'But the disguises only work at a distance, allowing you to get up close . . . and the guard upstairs was small and easy to knock out.'

Argon nodded. 'And considering that man's

58

neck is thicker than my waist and his chin is practically missing, I don't think—'

'Shh! Quiet!' Olu rasped suddenly, turning to Gladius with his eyes bright and a wide smile on his face. 'I've got a really good idea. Listen: you need to take your uniform off!'

'But then—'

'Come on! It's getting light outside – we're all going to end up prisoners if we're not careful!'

The door to the kitchens, which always hung open slightly to allow the steam to escape, burst open and slammed against the wall.

Gladius flew into the room, face first, landed heavily on the stones and rolled over with a tortured scream, clutching his stomach. He was back in his own grubby tunic.

Before the giant cook could shift his immense bulk in reaction to the intrusion, Argon and Olu charged into the room. They were both still dressed head to foot in the uniform of D'Tong's guards.

Without paying any attention to the cook, who was still attempting to struggle out from behind the table, they immediately laid into Gladius. Argon aimed several well-acted kicks at the stomach of the big slave, while Olu used a staff he'd found in the corridor to viciously jab his friend in the small of the back.

'N? gàn ma?' the cook shouted, apparently confused as to whether he should intervene or assist them. 'N? gàn ma!'

Olu grumbled back at the giant, but not in any voice loud enough to be audible. Argon simply snatched Gladius by the neck, dragged him to his feet and charged across the room with him, hurling him headlong through the archway and down the long flight of steps beyond. Then he let out a roar of fake laughter and hurried down the steps after Gladius.

Olu muttered anew and, keeping his head down, followed the pair.

The enormous cook watched

them go, gave a heavy shrug, which sent jelly-like rumbles through his entire frame, and slumped back on to the bench.

Argon and Olu dashed down to the foot of the steps, where Gladius was lying in very real agony. He had bruises up and down his arms from the fall, and his face and hands were bleeding.

'I'm sorry,' Argon whispered. 'It had to look convincing.'

Gladius moaned slightly, as Olu helped to lift him on to his feet.

'It's not your fault, Argon,' he managed, through bloodied lips. 'You didn't actually kick me once, and you weren't to know the steps were directly behind the arch. Come on; let's move.'

The passage before them was cold and dank, and the walls glistened with moisture. Torches flamed from heavy braziers that had been driven into the stones with long iron nails. The flickering light lent the dungeons a million shadows and a real sense of danger.

Argon and Olu proceeded slowly through each tunnel, with Gladius limping along behind them. The passages all seemed very twisty, and for a long time there wasn't a door or a window or anything that suggested the place was still in regular use. It was only when they reached the head of another long flight of stone steps that Argon began to realize how massive the Winter Palace really was.

'We must be below sea level, here,' said the Gaul, who snatched a torch from one of the braziers to light their way as they moved down into the darkness. 'I mean, the palace is set in a valley as it is, and I reckon we must have gone down a fair way . . .'

The new corridor was rough looking, as if the tunnel had been hewn from the stone and then simply abandoned. Gladius thought it was exactly the sort of cave network you would find in an underground mine, and said as much to the others. There were a lot of large niches, as if the caves were in the process of being extended.

'In fact, I can't imagine the cells are too—'

'Shhh!'

It was Olu who had sounded the alarm. He

grabbed hold of Argon's shoulder and squeezed it, tightly.

'There's movement up ahead! Into that niche; quickly! Put out that torch!'

The trio bundled themselves inside the small alcove and waited.

Sure enough, the shadows in the passageway were lengthening, and torchlight approached. The sound of footsteps was also clearly audible, now, echoing louder and louder as a familiar voice rang out in the corridor.

'Your men did well, D'Tong. You may consider your bargain fulfilled. My ship is waiting; we leave in the morning. I see no reason to linger while the boy recovers from his injuries. He will suffer much worse when he returns to my land.'

Olu had to clap a hand over his mouth to stifle a cough as Slavious Doom and King D'Tong strode past, surrounded by a group of guards. Argon and Gladius both squatted down in the niche, making every effort to hold their breath.

'It is regrettable that one of your ninjas was killed, but I am not entirely surprised: I did warn you that the slaves were dangerous. Did your men recover the other two?'

'Indeed, Doom Lord. They sleep, still.'

The voices echoed along the corridor, and Gladius peered out of the niche to watch the party ascend the great staircase that led to the sub-basement. The light died away with them.

'We need to move quickly,' Argon snapped. 'And we have to find another torch – we can't pick our way through this maze in the pitch dark.'

'I don't think we'll need to,' Gladius replied, grabbing the Gaul's chin and turning his head to face the staircase. 'There's someone else coming, now; from the other direction!'

Sure enough, a pool of light was advancing on them from the end of the passage. This time, however, it surrounded a rough brute of a man who seemed to carry as much muscle as the cook carried fat. He was naked from the waist up, and a heavy ring of keys jangled from a belt that surrounded his loincloth. In one hand he carried the torch; the other held a plate of stale-looking bread.

The boys waited until this newcomer had sauntered past before creeping from the alcove, following at a distance.

'That has to be the jailer,' Olu whispered. 'But he's one of Doom's men, not the king's.'

Argon shrugged. 'Maybe Doom doesn't trust D'Tong to keep Decimus under lock and key.'

'He can trust him all right,' said Gladius,

uneasily. 'He has more muscles than you, Argon.'

Doom's jailer moved on through the network of passages, the spluttering torch held high above him. Eventually, he reached a heavy iron door for which, after several failed attempts, he located the correct key. There was a resounding click, and the jailer hauled open the door, depositing his torch on a bracket in the corridor before disappearing from view.

'Now!' Gladius hissed, hurrying forward. Argon and Olu overtook him in an effort to reach the iron door before it creaked closed behind him again.

There, stretching out beyond the door, was a vast chamber full of flaming braziers, heavy chains, and all manner of twisted, evil-looking torture equipment. It was a unique vision of hell.

The jailer was already halfway through the room. As the trio looked on, he marched straight past a young girl who was secured to the wall by a long chain with thick links that seemed to loop halfway around the chamber. There was also some poor, unfortunate soul locked in a cage that hung from the ceiling, but it was difficult to see how badly hurt or starved this creature was from the doorway.

The jailer walked underneath him, arriving beside a stone slab containing a figure that had to be Decimus. After all, it was evident that

Doom wanted the young gladiator to be kept alive and this man was bringing him food of a sort.

'Shall we hide in here until he's gone?' Argon whispered.

Gladius rolled his eyes. 'No – idiot – we need his keys! We'll have to kill him!'

Argon muttered under his breath, but it was Olu that made the first move. Uttering a silent prayer, the agile slave dashed forward and crossed the room in several gigantic strides. To their combined amazement, he hardly made a single noise, and quickly vanished into the shadows so stealthily that it almost beggared belief.

Even I can't see him, Gladius thought, and I know he's there.

Almost as if he sensed a pending attack, as he leaned over Decimus, the jailer suddenly dropped the plate he was carrying and spun around.

Gladius, acting mainly on instinct, dashed out into the corridor and snatched the torch from the wall bracket. Then, holding the flaming beacon aloft, he marched straight into the dungeon room and began to wave it around, immediately grabbing the man's attention. Argon stood beside him, cupping both hands around his mouth and shouting challenges to the surprised jailer, who made straight for the pair with a grim determination.

'That's right!' Argon screamed. 'Let's see how tough you are!'

Even as the Gaul strode forward to meet his

opponent, Gladius saw Olu stalking up behind
him. The slave took a running jump and leapt
on the man's back, just as Argon hurtled into
him from the front. However, for once the group
had dangerously underestimated their

73

opposition. Instead of crashing to the ground, as expected, the muscular Roman simply dived forward, hurling Olu over his head and sending the slave crashing into Argon. The Gaul raised both hands in order to catch his friend but the result was a sprawling disaster for both of them. Laughing with apparent delight, the jailer placed a hefty boot into Olu's spine and stamped on one of Argon's ankles, causing the Gaul to scream out in pain. Then, as if the attack had been merely a distraction, the jailer returned his attention to Gladius and exploded forward in a sprint.

Gladius only had time to drop the torch he was carrying before the jailer cannoned into him. The pair tumbled to the ground as Gladius tried desperately to defend himself from a rain of heavy punches.

'He's tough,' Argon admitted, scrambling to his feet. 'I'm going to help Gladius.'

'Go for it,' Olu panted, jumping up with a smile. 'I snatched the big oaf's keys before he threw me.'

As Argon hurtled towards the fight in the doorway, Olu retreated to the back of the chamber and set to work on the manacles securing Decimus to the slab. The young gladiator was barely conscious, and didn't seem fully aware of the situation until Olu had all but freed him from the chains.

'You took your time,' he said, wincing with pain as he swung his wounded body around and lifted himself off the slab.

'Don't mention it,' Olu muttered, turning his

attention to the cage swinging overhead. 'Shall we try to release that poor—'

Olu froze as his gaze fell upon Teo.

'T-T-Teo? No – it can't be ... that's impossible. I saw you—'

Decimus shook the slave from his reverie.

'No time for that,' Decimus warned, pointing across the chamber. 'Gladius and Argon are having serious trouble with that jailer, and I'm going to help them. You get Teo out of the cage and free the girl.'

Argon was quickly realizing that he would rather spend a day fighting an entire pack of ninjas than spend another second fighting the jailer. As yet another iron fist crashed into his jaw, the Gaul staggered backwards and tumbled on to the ground.

Gladius was quick to assist his fallen friend, leaping at the jailer and, once again, using all of his weight to try to force the man off his feet. It didn't work, and a swift knee caught him. Gladius crumpled, and the jailer drove a boot into his jaw, knocking him unconscious. A sidelong glance informed the jailer that Argon was trying to get up, but a second well-aimed

boot sent the Gaul off to dreamland, too. He grinned at his handiwork, spat on the ground and slowly turned around.

Decimus Rex was standing before him, fists clenched and a determined look on his face.

'You're wounded in three places,' sneered the jailer, noticing his missing keys for the first time. 'If it wasn't for Doom's orders, I'd kill you where you stand. Get back on the slab.'

Decimus nodded. 'Try to put me there,' he said.

The jailer shrugged, and charged forward. The first punch he threw was wildly off target, and Decimus moved in to capitalize on the mistake. When he threw one of his own, however, a pain shot along his side and practically doubled him up. He was still reeling from the shock when his opponent kicked his legs out from under him and dropped the young gladiator straight on to his back.

Decimus screamed with the pain of the assault, but gritted his teeth and immediately tried to get up again. His strength failed him, however, and a second wave of agony washed over him. It was like fighting two opponents, and his own body was by far the fiercer. He felt himself snatched by the hair and half dragged on to his feet.

'Only an idiot would try to fight in your condition,' the jailer growled. 'I don't know why Doom thinks you are so impor—'

The sentence was never finished: Decimus saw the merest glimpse of movement, and then

the man simply flew backwards as if he had been hit by a bag of bricks.

'Olu?'

Decimus peered around in his weakened state, looking for his other companions ... but both Olu and Teo were standing, open-mouthed, watching the event.

Princess Akina, now out of her chains, had stepped forward and delivered some sort of kick that caught the big jailer completely by surprise.

She stepped forward, calmly and deliberately, waiting for the man to get up again.

Sure enough, he clambered to his feet ... but it took him a few seconds to focus on the girl and realize what had happened.

Then he lunged forward. He threw a punch,

which missed, a kick that was glanced aside and a third, double-handed strike that, to the group's utter astonishment, was actually blocked, broken open and twisted against him. There were two sickening cracks as the princess splintered a bone in the man's arm and drove his legs out from under him in exactly the same move he himself had used on Decimus only moments before. Then she leapt into the air in a manner that suggested some sort of beautiful, elegant dance before she landed with an absolutely devastating chop to his throat.

The jailer convulsed on the floor, coughing and spluttering for several seconds. Then he was still.

A deathly silence settled on the room.

As they slowly came round, Gladius and

Argon both took one look at Teo and felt sure they were still dreaming.

Decimus just stared up at Akina with a look of complete and total bewilderment.

'I thought you were a princess?' he said.

In the shadows, Teo smiled.

CHAPTER IV

THE TRAP

'Teo! You're alive!'

Gladius got to his feet and then, almost immediately, fell over again. Argon clambered up behind him, his eyes awash with sudden emotion as the full enormity of the situation sank in.

'H-how did you—'

'LATER!'

The booming voice of Decimus Rex rang out in the dungeon like a bell chime. Still wincing with pain, the young gladiator struggled on to his knees, gratefully accepting Olu's help when it was offered. 'We need to get out of here now . . . before Doom realizes there's something wrong.'

Gladius and Argon both shook their heads at the same time.

'We'll never get back past that monster in the kitchens,' said Olu, carefully supporting his friend. 'Argon, Gladius and I tricked our way down here, but if we try to get out with you, Teo and . . .' he paused and glanced respectfully at Akina, 'the princess, we'll all end up plastered to the wall.'

The group released a collective sigh, and even the resourceful Gladius seemed to be fresh out of ideas. It was Teo who shattered the depressed silence, and when he spoke, the gathered slaves gasped in astonishment: the little prisoner hadn't uttered so much as a mumble during most of his time at the arena.

'Kitchens,' he said, 'not only way. D'Tong passage through wall.'

Teo pointed at the entrance to the dungeon

room, and the group immediately followed
him as he hurried towards the entrance.
Despite his capture and confinement, he
moved every bit as fast as he had in the arena
during the agility trials.

Emerging into the corridor, Teo moved off
to the right before heading down a new,
partially concealed tunnel that Decimus
thought looked just like the rest of the wall
section. It was deep, sloping and covered in a
layer of fine sand. Eventually, they arrived at a
dead end, where the little prisoner dropped on
to his knees and began to feel around in the
sand, as if he'd lost something incredibly
valuable and was searching for it by touch.

At length, his hand found a metal ring in the
sand, and he pulled on it with all his might.

When nothing seemed to be happening, Argon joined him on the floor and lent his greater strength to the attempt.

Finally, there was a heavy 'clink' and the dead-end wall swung back on an ancient, powerful hinge that creaked loudly in the dark. A flight of steps beyond the door led down to yet another lower level. Teo led the way, and the group hurried after him. Argon held aloft the torch he'd snatched from the dungeon, bathing them all in a soft pool of light.

'So . . .' Decimus said, glancing at Akina as Olu helped him along the new tunnel. 'You're royalty, then? Yes? An actual princess?'

He felt his face flush when Akina smiled at him in the torchlight.

'Princess,' she said, in a voice so small and gentle that he nearly forgot it came from the same girl who had all but killed the Roman jailer.

'Impressive fighting,' he added, motioning to Gladius, who performed an impromptu impression of her kick.

Akina smiled an acknowledgement, but said nothing more.

'Arrive!'

Teo stopped at a small side door, and opened it carefully. A new flight of steps became visible, but this set went up ... a long, long way up.

Decimus thought he saw the tiniest pinprick of daylight in the distance.

'Way out,' Teo confirmed. 'We go.'

The group began to ascend the stairs, Teo and Argon leading while Olu supported Decimus at the back. Akina and Gladius were in the middle, Gladius being careful to keep his distance from the princess in case he accidentally stepped on her heel.

After climbing for some ten or twenty minutes, Teo arrived at a heavy wooden door that was barred on the inside. Light spilled out all around it.

Argon handed the torch to Gladius and lifted the bar from its hinges. Together, he and Teo pushed open the door and stepped out into the daylight.

'Free!' Teo shouted, jumping for joy before his feet even touched the soft, green grass of the Winter Palace grounds.

Argon closed his eyes and took a deep breath as the cold air hit his face.

Akina hopped over the threshold, stepping aside as Gladius stumbled out after her. Finally, Olu half carried a tired and noticeably weak Decimus Rex out into the light.

The young gladiator rested heavily on his friend.

'Thank the fates,' he breathed. 'Now we need to get to Tonino's boat ... and fas—'

He stopped speaking when he realized that Gladius, Akina, Teo and Argon all stood around him, frozen to the spot. He felt Olu's grip on him tighten, and looked up to see what was causing the sudden panic.

There, standing in the centre of the palace garden, was Slavious Doom. The towering overlord was surrounded by a small horde of guards, both Roman and Chinese, and King D'Tong stood beside him with a dark smirk on his lined face. The two surviving ninjas, Tekaro and Miriki, were both visible at the right hand of their king, but Decimus's eyes were drawn not to them, but to the young figure standing at the left hand of Doom himself.

Ruma stepped forward, clapping his hands as if he was genuinely pleased to see his friends.

The scrawny Etrurian spoke with such joy in his voice that it took a second for them to properly hear what he was saying, and even longer to understand why the enemy was allowing him to speak at all.

'Amazing!' Ruma cried. 'The great Decimus Rex escapes once again, leading all his idiot friends into even greater peril for no good reason. I see you've even picked up some local help along the way.'

Ruma's gaze took in Akina, but skipped over Teo as if his mind wasn't ready to deal with the fact that he recognized him.

'Ruma!' Gladius cried, his face a mask of horror. 'What in the name of the gods are you doing?'

'It's the dust!' Olu shouted, at his side. 'That

dust turned your mind—'

'I've had enough of you all!' the Etrurian screamed. 'Ever since I met you, my life has been in ruins. Well, not any more – I've struck a deal with Lord Doom, and I'm going home FREE. All I need to do is clap you all in chains, and I'll be rid of you once and for all.'

Ruma jumped down from the little hillock he was standing on and made directly for the group, Tekaro, Miriki and several guards leaping after him.

The sound of Slavious Doom's haunting cackle echoed around the hills.

'Ruma!' Decimus screamed, suddenly pushing Olu aside and marching to the front of the group, the pain from his wounds drowned by the strength of his anger. 'If you take one more step . . . I will make you wish you had never been born.'

The Etrurian hesitated, his eyes suddenly awash with crimson tears of terrible confusion. For a moment, Decimus thought – and hoped – that whatever poisoning influence Olu had mentioned was wearing off.

Then Ruma screamed out a battle cry . . . and charged.

COMING SOON

As the skies darken over Yelang and a terrible rainstorm drenches the land, Decimus and the other slaves must conquer the storm raging in their own hearts. Betrayed by a friend and ensnared by the evil Slavious Doom, they find themselves once again in a battle to survive. Can Ruma be saved from the terrible insanity inflicted on him by the red mist, or will he need to be defeated in order for the slaves to escape? Find out now in . . .

THE WHITE SNAKE

GLADIATOR GAME
AVOIDING THE COOK

In the book, Olu and Argon avoid the monstrous cook by pretending Gladius is their prisoner. However, in this game the object is simply to reach the dungeon door BEFORE the cook reaches YOU!

Pictured on the following pages are two grids, one containing an overhead picture of the kitchen and one containing letters and numbers.

One player takes the part of a prisoner and one takes on the role of the cook. Both starting points are marked. The prisoner must reach the dungeon door before the cook reaches the prisoner.

Deciding who goes first – it really doesn't matter as both players move their characters at the same time – each player takes it in turns to close their eyes and poke a pencil or fingernail randomly into the second grid. Then, they must move their pieces (you can use counters or just mark your move with a pencil) the allotted number of spaces.

So . . . a result of C_1/P_3 means the cook can move one space through the first grid, while the prisoner moves three. Good luck! Remember to swap characters after each game – it is more fun that way!

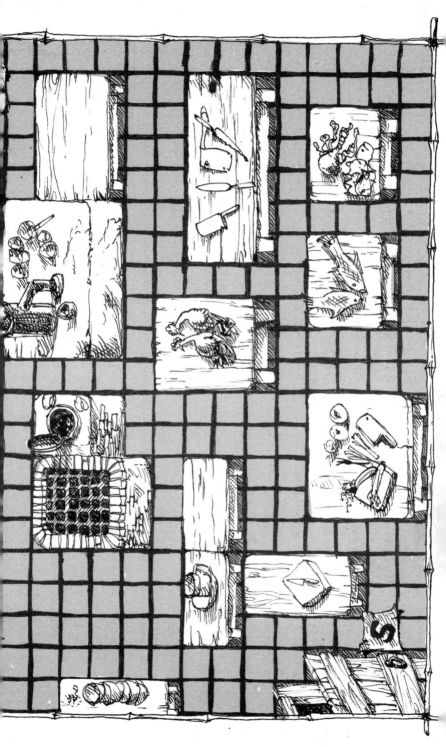

SEARCH GRID

C1/P1	C1/P1	C1/P1	C1/P1	C1/P1	C1/P1	C1/P1	C1/P1
C1/P1	C5/P6	C5/P5	C4/P2	C5/P5	C5/P6	C5/P5	C4/P2
C1/P1	C6/P5	C3/P4	C5/P6	C3/P4	C6/P5	C3/P4	C5/P6
C1/P1	C2/P4	C4/P3	C3/P4	C4/P3	C2/P4	C4/P3	C3/P4
C1/P1	C4/P2	C2/P8	C8/P2	C2/P8	C4/P2	C2/P8	C8/P2
C1/P1	C1/P1	C1/P1	C1/P1	C1/P1	C1/P1	C1/P1	C1/P1

C1/P1	C2/P8	C4/P3	C3/P4	C5/P5	C1/P1
C1/P1	C4/P2	C2/P4	C6/P5	C5/P6	C1/P1
C1/P1	C2/P8	C4/P3	C3/P4	C5/P5	C1/P1
C1/P1	C2/P8	C4/P3	C3/P4	C5/P5	C1/P1
C1/P1	C4/P2	C2/P4	C6/P5	C5/P6	C1/P1
C1/P1	C2/P8	C4/P3	C3/P4	C5/P5	C1/P1
C1/P1	C1/P1	C1/P1	C1/P1	C1/P1	C1/P1

CHARACTER PROFILE
AKINA

NAME: Akina

FROM: The Summer Palace, China

HEIGHT: 1.63 metres

BODY TYPE: Lean, slender

Fact File:
* Uses a special spinning kick as her main attack.
* Was captured by Slavious Doom's men for King D'Tong
* Is the only daughter of a king who rules the land neighbouring Yelang, on its western border.

AKINA QUIZ: How well do you know Akina? Can you answer the following three questions?

1. WHAT IS THE FIRST WORD AKINA SAYS TO DECIMUS?

2. WHO DOES AKINA DEFEAT IN HAND-TO-HAND COMBAT?

3. WHO IS AFRAID OF STEPPING ON THE PRINCESS'S HEEL?

Answers: 1. Teo, p.31 2. The Roman Jailer, p.82 3. Gladius, p.92

HOW MANY OF

GLADIATOR BOY

SERIES TWO HAVE YOU COLLECTED?

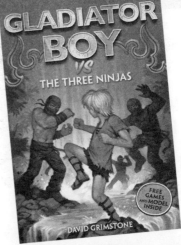

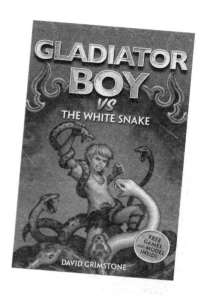

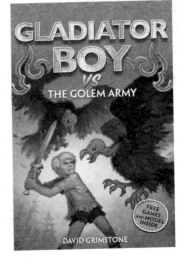

GLADIATOR BOY

WWW.GLADIATORBOY.COM

Have you checked out the Gladiator Boy website?
It's the place to go for games, downloads,
activities, sneak previews and lots of fun!

Sign up to the newsletter at
WWW.GLADIATORBOY.COM
and receive exclusive extra
content and the opportunity
to enter special members-only
competitions.